BOOK ONE

City Cousin

Chapter 1 Ghosts in the House 2
Chapter 2 Bright Morning 8
Chapter 3 What Should I Call Her? 16
Chapter 4 Another Ghost 24

Written by Katherine Rawson
Illustrated by Steven Petruccio

PIONEER VALLEY EDUCATIONAL PRESS, INC.

Chapter 1
Ghosts in the House

Anna got out of bed quietly.
She tried not to wake her little cousin Sophie.
She tiptoed to the window
and looked out across the yard.
The barn looked like a great black shadow
against the starry sky.
All was dark and quiet.

Anna thought about Mama and Papa at home.
It seemed so long since she had seen them,
but it was just this morning that they waved
good-bye to her at the train station in Boston.

The train ride took all day. As the train chugged along, Anna thought about all the fun she would have at her uncle's farm in Vermont.

"It will be good for you to get out of the hot city," Mama had said. Everyone was scared after the heat wave of last August.

Uncle Al and cousin Harry met her
at Deer River station in the farm wagon
and drove her over bumpy roads
to Maple Tree Farm.

Anna had been excited about spending the summer
with family, but now everything
seemed so strange and far from home.
Boston streets were filled with buildings
and horses and noise.
Everything was so quiet here.

Suddenly a shadow darted across the yard.

Anna looked around.

What was it? Anna's heart pounded.

Then she heard it.

"Hoo-hoo-hoo-hoo!"

Ghosts! Anna flew back to the bed.

She heard it again.

"Hoo-hoo-hoo-hoo!"

Anna held her breath. Then she heard something else.

Scratch, scratch, scratch.

Ghosts right there in the bedroom!
Anna dove under the covers and snuggled
close to the sleeping Sophie.

Chapter 2
Bright Morning

When Anna woke up, she was alone in the bed. Sunlight filled the room.
She could hear voices and clanking dishes from the kitchen below.
Anna jumped out of bed, pulled on her dress, and hurried downstairs.

She found Aunt Polly frying something on the stove. Harry and Sophie sat at the table eating their breakfast. Uncle Al was just coming through the door with an armload of wood.

"Did you sleep well?" he asked.

"Yes," said Anna. "Finally! But it took a while because of the ghosts."

"Ghosts?" Harry laughed.

"Didn't you hear them?" said Anna.
"They sounded like this." She tried to make the sound she had heard in the night.

"Like this?" said Uncle Al.

"Hoo-hoo-hoo-hoo!"

"Yes!" said Anna. "You heard them too!"

"That's just a Barred Owl," said Harry. "Don't you have owls in Boston?"

"I guess not," said Anna. Then she said, "Do owls make a noise like this?"

She scratched the tabletop.

"You're just making stuff up now," said Harry.

Aunt Polly hugged Anna and glared at Harry. "I'm sure Anna's seen plenty of things in Boston that you know nothing about." She placed a plate of pancakes and a glass of milk in front of Anna. "That's milk fresh from our cows," she said.

"From your cows?" said Anna. "Really?"

"You do know that milk comes from cows, don't you?" laughed Harry.

"Of course I know that!" said Anna. "I guess I just never thought about it. At home, the milk is delivered to our door in glass bottles."

"It's delivered to our door too," said Harry. "But not in bottles. Our milk is delivered right inside the cow!"

This time Anna laughed right along with Harry.

Chapter 3
What Should I Call Her?

After breakfast, Harry said,
"Come on, Anna. I'll show you around the barn."

Anna followed Harry across the yard
and into the big red barn.
Inside, the large room was dark
and damp, and there were no animals in sight.

"Where are the cows?" asked Anna.

"In the pasture," said Harry.
"We'll bring them back this afternoon for milking."
He pointed to a ladder built into the wall.
"Let's go look at the hayloft."

Anna followed Harry up the ladder
to a large, open space. Loose hay
covered the floor, and sunlight
poured though an open door.
Suddenly, something grey and white ran by.
Anna jumped.

"What was that?"

"Oh, that's just Shadow," said Harry.
"The barn cat. She's a great mouse catcher."

Anna heard a soft mewing.
She looked down to see a little ball of white fur climbing out of the hay at her feet.

"That's the last of Shadow's kittens," Harry explained. "The one we couldn't give away."

Anna scooped up the cat and cuddled it in her arms.
"I wish she were mine!" she said.
"Maybe Aunt Polly will let me have her."

Back at the house, Aunt Polly said,
"Of course you can have the cat.
I know you'll take good care of her."

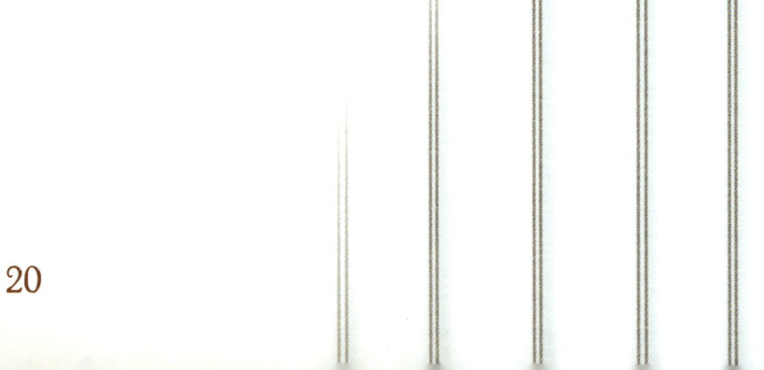

"What should I call her?" Anna wondered.

"Milky," said Sophie. "Because she's white like milk."

"Even though she didn't come in a bottle," laughed Harry.

Anna stroked the cat's back.
"Hello, Milky," she said.
But the cat jumped off her lap
and ran across the room.

"I guess that's not her name," she said.
Anna looked around. "Where did she go?"

The cat had disappeared.

Chapter 4
Another Ghost

By bedtime, the cat still hadn't returned.

"I'm worried," said Anna.

"What if the ghosts get her?"

"I bet she went back to the barn," said Uncle Al.

"Shadow will take care of her."

Anna lay awake for a long time that night.
She was worried about her cat.
The next morning she was up early.
"I have to look for my kitty," she explained.
"Breakfast first," said Aunt Polly.

Anna sat down at the table. "I heard that scratching sound again last night," she said. "You know. The ghosts."

Harry laughed so hard that milk squirted out of his mouth. Aunt Polly frowned.
"Eat your breakfast, Harry," she said.

Then Anna heard something.

"Meow, meow."

She looked down. "My kitty!" she exclaimed, bending down to pick it up. "Oh no!" She dropped the cat.
"She has something in her mouth."

Harry looked. "It's just a mouse," he said. He carried the dead animal to the door and threw it outside.

"Why did she bring me that disgusting thing?" said Anna.

"She's just doing her job," said Aunt Polly. "Mice eat the grain we use to feed our animals. The cats help us keep the mice away."

"And it looks like the cat got your ghost," said Uncle Al.

Anna frowned. "What do you mean?"

"The scratching sound you heard was probably that mouse."

Anna brightened. "What a smart kitty!" she said. "She catches mice *and* ghosts. And now I know what to call her." She leaned toward the cat. "Here, Ghost!" she called.

The cat jumped up on her lap,
and Anna stroked her white fur.
"We're going to have a great summer
at Maple Tree Farm!" she said.

Ghost purred.